Koala and the Flower

Mary Murphy

ROARING BROOK PRESS
Brookfield, Connecticut

Badger and Raccoon see things in black and white.
They are always sure that they are always right.
Little gray Koala isn't sure about
many things. She asks lots
of questions.

Badger knows that Badger is right.

Raccoon knows that Raccoon is right.

And they
both know
that they know
much more than Koala.

One day, Koala goes for a walk.

She goes slowly, looking at things from all sides.

She finds something new. It is a yellow flower.

Koala has never

seen a yellow

flower before,

except in a picture.

Koala runs all the way home…

"Guess what I saw!" she says.
"A yellow flower! Come and see!"

But Badger and Raccoon are too busy.

Koala picks the flower

and brings it home.

"**Where** do flowers come from?" she asks.

Badger and Raccoon are sure they know.

Koala puts the flower in a jar so that she can look at it.

She doesn't know that flowers need water.

The flower dies.

"Poor flower!" says Koala.

"I should have left you where you were."

MAKING FLOWERS (by Raccoon)

1.

Raccoon shows Koala
how to make flowers.

2.

They get paper and wire
and string and glue.

3.

They cut and twist
and tie and stick.

4.

But it doesn't turn out right.
"You did it wrong," says Raccoon.

MAKING FLOWERS (by Badger)

1. "Badger, how do we get flowers?" "Easy! We bake them"

Badger shows Koala how to make flowers.

2.

They get flour and milk and sugar and butter.

3.

They sift and stir and roll and bake.

4. "Never mind"

But it doesn't turn out right. "You did it wrong," says Badger.

Koala goes for another walk with some flower cookies in her backpack.

She walks and walks and walks. She goes farther than sh

as ever gone before.

She meets a little gray donkey. (He looks very big to Koala.)

Koala tells him about her flower.

"I don't know how to make flowers," says Donkey.

"But there is a place I go when I want to find out things."

Donkey gives Koala a lift...

...all the way...

...to...

Koala didn't know there were so many books in the world. She didn't know there were so many animals trying to find out things. She didn't know that most animals know that they don't know everything.

"This is great!" she says.

Koala goes home with a backpack full of books.

She reads…

…and reads.

Koala buys some seeds.

"Now I can make some flowers," she says.

She shakes seeds from her own beloved flower too.

Badger and Raccoon snigger. They laugh when she

digs a patch in a sunny part of the yard.

They guffaw when she puts the seeds on the ground and covers them with earth.

They roll around when she sprinkles water on the seeds.

But Koala doesn't care.

Koala reads her library books and waits for her seeds to grow. Sometimes the sun shines…

And sometimes clouds bring rain.

After a few days, little green spikes poke out of the earth. Koala tends the flower patch. She carries snails away.

She waters the earth. Soon little buds appear on top of the little green spikes. Time goes by and…

...this is what happens.

"Come and see!" says Koala to Badger and Raccoon.

"Well done!" says Badger. "Just what I expected."

"Me too!" says Raccoon. "First rate!"

"I knew it!" says Koala. "I knew it would work!"

Now Koala knows about lots of flowers, and insects, and colors.

"It's still like magic," she says…

"…at least that's what I think!"